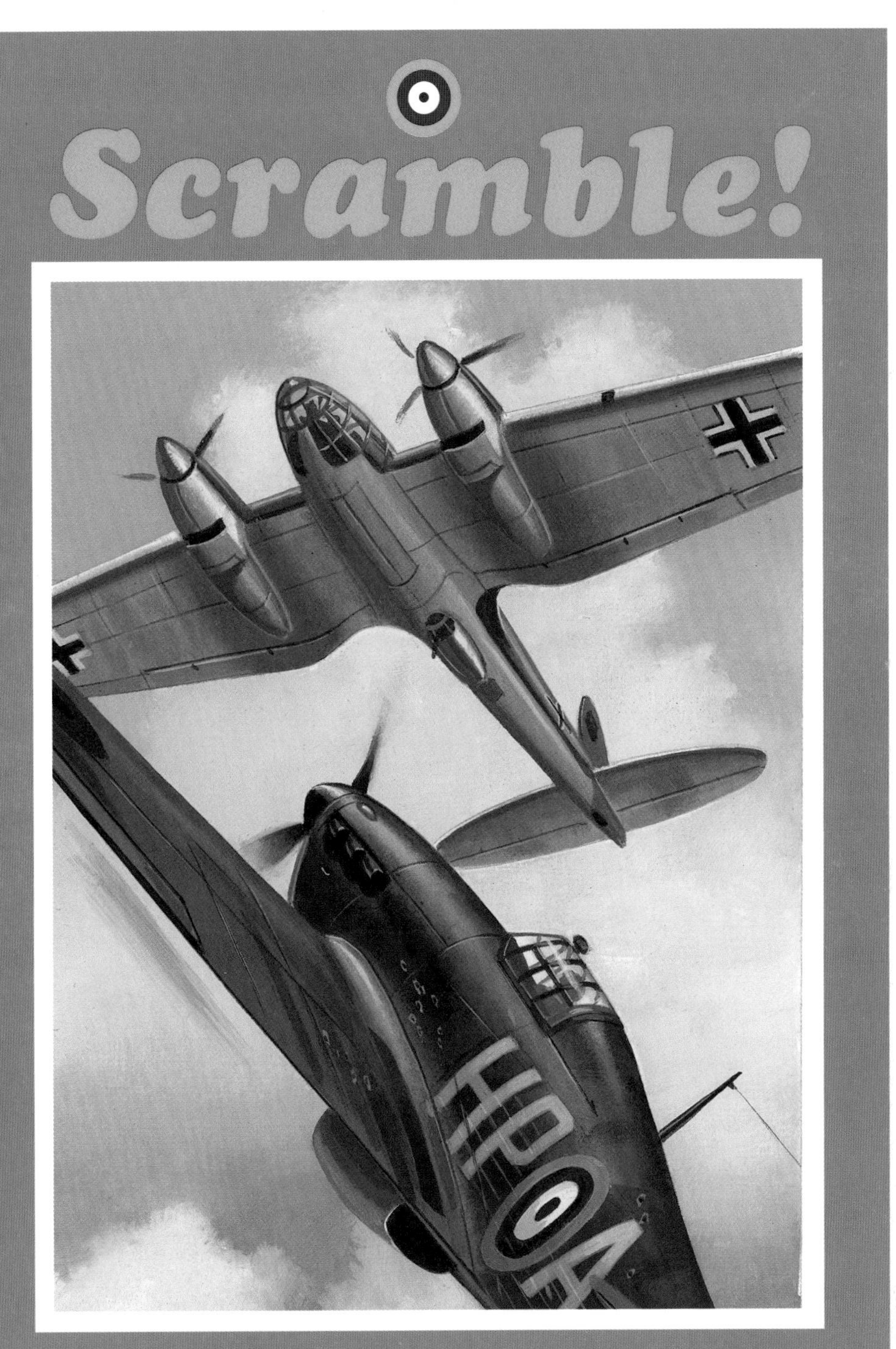

Scramble!

By DON PATTERSON

Illustrated by Sonny S

ISBN 1-929031-00-9
Library of Congress 99-95202

Printed in the U.S.A.
First Hindsight™ printing, June 1999

PICTURE CREDITS
Many thanks to the following organizations for giving permission to reprint illustrations and text used in the "In Hindsight" section of this book:
p.67- The RAF at War. Time Life Books, The Epic of Flight Series, Chicago IL.
Courtesy of Imperial War Museum.
pp.70-71- Hurricane Aces 1939-40. Osprey Aircraft of the Aces,
Reed Books Limited, London. Courtesy of Tony Holmes.

Written by Don Patterson
Illustrated by Sonny Schug/Studio West
Edited by Mary Parenteau
Production by Kline/Phoenix Advertising Graphics

To My Son.

What's Important To Me?

You Are, Mr. Ian Patterson.

TABLE OF CONTENTS

"SCRAMBLE!"

CHAPTER ONE

A RAINY DAY IN HAMPTON

Rain continued to pour on the fields of Hampton county for the third straight day. Since most people took shelter from the bad weather, a still quiet settled over the gray, English countryside. As bleak as it was, the cold and rain couldn't keep young Harry Winslow from visiting his special friends. But now it was time for him to return home. Trudging back along the muddy path between his house and the hedgerow fence that separated the Winslow farm from its neighbor, Hampton Airfield, Harry pulled his thin coat tightly around his small shoulders. A British Royal Air Force base, Hampton field had been built three years earlier in anticipation of war.

Soaked to the skin, Harry ran the last hundred yards to the front porch of the Winslow house. His light brown hair was matted and rain dripped down his face.

Upon reaching the first step, Harry stomped the mud from his worn boots and kicked them off before sprinting up the remaining stairs to go inside.

"Is that you, love?" Mrs. Winslow called from the kitchen when she heard the front door quickly close.

"Yes Mother, it's just me," Harry replied and started to peel off his drenched, blue-gray coat.

"Harry, you need to stay inside on days like this or you'll catch a fever!" Harry's mother continued, her concerned voice growing closer as she stepped around the corner to join him.

Harry looked up at his mother and mumbled, "Three days of this weather. I can't stay inside forever!"

Mrs. Winslow smiled and helped her son struggle out of the dripping coat. "No dear, I guess you can't," she said with a loving tone. "But run up to your room now and get some dry clothes on before you get sick."

Just being around his mother made Harry feel a little warmer. Ever since his father had been commissioned to be a part of the British Intelligence and left to work in London, he had felt a sense of loneliness and apprehension. Mrs.

Winslow worked hard to soothe the emptiness in Harry's heart, but sometimes her efforts simply made him miss his father that much more. Reminded of his loneliness, Harry swallowed hard. To keep his mother from worrying, Harry reached over and gave her a damp hug, hiding the sad look on his face. Then he ran up the creaking stairs into his room at the top of the landing to change his soggy clothes.

Mrs. Winslow opened the hall closet to hang up her son's wet coat and thought, "I wonder if those RAF boys know just how important they are to him."

CHAPTER 2

THE HOLIDAY IS OVER

Pools of oily water on the hardstand of Hampton Airfield reflected the gray clouds sweeping across the sky above. Strangely enough, the Royal Air Force fighter pilots gathered in the barracks were in an upbeat and lively mood for such gloomy weather. The playful chatter of men passing time filled the air.

Sitting in a leather chair in a corner of the room, the Squadron Leader, Captain Ted Dawson, quietly thumbed through the pages of the current issue of "Stick and Rudder". Only his sandy hair could be seen over the top of the magazine. Dawson was so intent on the article he was reading, that even the noise from the other men couldn't break his concentration.

Across the room, seated at a small wooden table, Captain Simms and Lieutenant Gainey were in the middle of a rather loud game of checkers. Some of the other pilots played cards, and Lieutenant Hyatt, an art student before the war, sketched pictures of his friends and their activities in his sketch book. He quietly twirled a reddish pencil in his hand, looking questioningly at the sharp tip. The pencil color matched his unruly auburn hair. With short strokes, Hyatt used it to brighten the faces of the men in his drawing.

Although, typically, most people would be frustrated by day after day of rain, the men in the barracks were relaxed and playful. Then again, these were not typical times, and this was not a normal summer. This year, most of the world was at war. Now, and especially for these men, bad weather created some of the cheeriest moments. Adverse weather was the only thing that grounded the air forces of both sides, temporarily ending the fight that was otherwise an everyday life and death struggle.

"Say, by the way... Andy," Captain Dawson mumbled from behind the pages of his magazine. "Thanks for finding those lost buttons, and sewing them back on my dress uniform."

Captain Simms looked up from the checker-

"Both men began to survey the rest of the group..."

board and cocked his head to one side. In a confused voice he replied, "Well... you're very welcome Ted, but I didn't sew any buttons on your uniform." The oldest flyer in the squadron, thirty year old Andrew Simms always looked out for the other pilots and their well-being.

"If you didn't do it, who did?" Captain Dawson asked. Simms shrugged his shoulders. Both men began to survey the rest of the group, searching for who among them could have been responsible for the secret favor. After scanning the entire room, Dawson and Simms, once again, looked at each other with complete bewilderment and shrugged their shoulders. Leaving the question unanswered, Dawson returned to his reading, and Simms calculated his next move on the checkerboard.

Concentrating on the red and black squares of the game board, Simms laughed lightly when his opponent, Brian Gainey, shared his thoughts.

"One thing's for sure," Gainey said with authority, "we know it's not the enemy! I can't imagine why they would care how our uniforms look, especially when we send them packing!"

Suddenly, the barracks door swung back on

its hinges. The loud crack it made startled the men inside. Colonel Harrison, a career RAF man, crossed the threshold and stepped into the room, while brushing rain water from his blue-gray uniform. The jovial group of fighter pilots quickly rose to their feet and saluted their base commander.

"Listen up lads! The weather forecast predicts lifting clouds tonight and partly cloudy skies tomorrow," Harrison gruffly announced to the now intent crew of twelve fighter pilots. "My guess is we'll be back at it by noon."

With a quick salute, the Colonel turned and darted out of the barracks and back into the downpour. The lively air and party-like atmosphere followed him. Everyone knew Colonel Harrison was right, their short vacation would soon be over. By noon tomorrow, it was likely that every man in the fighter group would take to his Hawker Hurricane fighter plane and, once again, defend England from German air attack. It was also very likely that some of the brave men gathered in the room now, would not be alive to play cards or chat again tomorrow night. Without question, being a fighter pilot was dangerous business.

CHAPTER 3

"SCRAMBLE!"

The weather forecast could not have been more precise. Dawn broke to a spectacular sunrise. With blue sky overhead, Hampton Airfield filled with the sounds of flight mechanics and air crews readying fighter planes for the impending "scramble." The word scramble described the action most accurately. As incoming enemy planes were detected by English radar, Fighter Command Headquarters informed the individual RAF fighter squadrons of the enemy location and heading. At the sound of an alarm, fighter pilots would "scramble" to their planes and be airborne in minutes, flying to engage the incoming German aircraft and protect England.

Taking in the bright morning sun, Dawson, Simms, and most of the other pilots had gathered out on the airfield. Sitting in the grass, anxiously waiting for the scream of the scramble alarm, Simms looked at Captain Dawson. "Ted," he started, "I told you, I didn't sew the buttons on your uniform."

"I know that, Andy," Captain Dawson returned in a quick fashion.

"Then why did you polish my shoes?" questioned Simms.

"I didn't polish your shoes, old man!" Dawson shouted back.

Lieutenant Gainey jumped into the conversation, "My shoes were polished too! I came back to my bunk last night and there they were, sitting on the end of my bed, shined better than I had ever seen them before!"

Instantly, the entire group of pilots realized that all of their shoes had been shined, their uniforms brushed, and their quarters straighten-up. Lieutenant Hyatt added that even the pencils in his drawing kit had been sharpened.

"Gentleman," Squadron Leader Captain Ted Dawson announced, "we have a serious mystery on our hands." The rest of the pilots agreed, and spent much of the morning struggling to determine who was spending so much time secretly taking care of the

details in their lives.

"It must be one of the crew chiefs," said Captain Simms. "They've always taken care of our planes and now they're taking care of us."

"Nah," replied Captain Dawson bluntly. "Sergeant Pendleton keeps me in the air, but he would never sew buttons on my uniform or shine my shoes!"

"What about one of the field engineers?" asked Hyatt shyly.

"What would a field engineer have to gain by making a pilot happy?" Lieutenant Mathews snorted, in his low, grinding voice.

"Could it be Colonel Harrison?" Brian Gainey quickly blurted out.

The other pilots rolled their eyes and groaned at Gainey. Being the youngest pilot, Gainey was always doing and saying things that the others thought were rather idiotic.

Captain Dawson summed up the feelings of the rest of the pilots when he snapped back to the young Lieutenant, "You're mad, Gainey. Colonels don't shine shoes! Now everyone think it over, and don't say another thing about it unless you can prove it with facts!" The men went silent,

challenged to determine the identity of their mysterious ally.

The day wore on, and serious anticipation of the "scramble" alarm settled over the entire airfield. Meanwhile, the tension grew as thick as the humid air, and by afternoon the pilots couldn't concentrate on the baffling mystery any longer.

Out on the hardstand, a mechanic dropped his tool kit, and the rattle of the tools scattering across the ground brought the pilots and air crew to their feet.

"Get a handle on it, lad!" echoed across the

field from someone chastising the man for his simple mistake.

Just as the mechanic picked up the last screwdriver, the scream of the "scramble" alarm pierced the air. In seconds, the whole airfield came alive with people rushing to their appointed stations. Air crews turned over the engines of the fighters. Scurrying pilots ran to the awaiting planes and jumped into the cockpits. Command officers made their way to the control room in order to provide vital information for the waves of fighter planes beginning to proceed down the runway. The thundering sound on the field was deafening as each fighter plane throttled up for take off. Plane after plane leapt to the sky.

Within minutes, the entire 14th Squadron was airborne, the planes quickly climbing away from those still left on the ground. Then the field grew quiet again. Up in the sky, the twelve assembling Hawker Hurricanes shrank to small points as their distance from Hampton Airfield increased.

Hearing the roar of the engines, Harry Winslow ran to his bedroom window and held his breath as he watched the squadron disappear.

CHAPTER 4

NORTHEAST FOR INTERCEPT

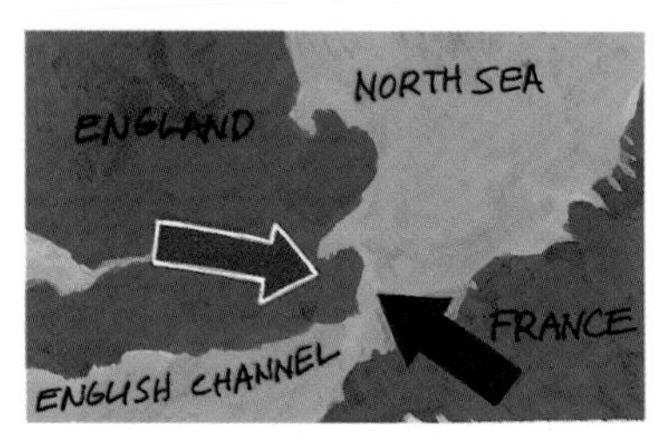

Instinctively, the squadron formed up on their commander, Captain Ted Dawson flying in the lead plane. Dawson was one of the best pilots in the Royal Air Force. Not only was he an exceptional pilot, he commanded his squadron in a way that achieved more victories with fewer losses than any other squadron in the entire RAF. Flying with Dawson practically insured the other pilots of coming home safely after a mission.

Just to the right of Dawson in their formation, was the veteran, Captain Andrew Simms. Simms, the oldest pilot in the Squadron, was second in command. The other, younger, pilots thought of Simms as the "Father of the 14th." When Simms gave an order, the response was more often "Roger, Old Chap," rather than the usual "Yes, sir!" As second in command, Captain

Simms would assume leadership of the squadron and the pilots on the outside chance that anything were to happen to Dawson.

The other ten planes in the formation with Dawson and Simms were flown by young men from throughout England, including Lieutenant Brian Gainey. Rumor had it that young Gainey lied about his age when he enlisted to become a pilot. He was quite impulsive and always mischievous, as witnessed by the pranks he continually played on the other members of the squadron. In spite of his youthful enthusiasm, Gainey had proven himself a born flyer many times over, often by saving the lives of his fellow pilots.

Captain Dawson leaned forward in order to look down the row of RAF fighter planes and keyed his radio. "All right gentlemen, the vacation is over. It's time for us to get back to work." Using his typical matter-of-fact tone, he continued, "Radar has the enemy formation and Control says it looks like they're heading for London. On my lead, follow northeast for intercept!"

"Roger!" replied the rest of the squadron.

From the corner of his eye, Dawson could

see Simms adjust his goggles. Simms looked to his left and flashed Dawson the thumbs-up sign. Dawson nodded to Simms in response. Then, with a slight push of the yoke, Captain Dawson angled his Hurricane to the northeast. Throttling up his engine, he increased his speed in order for the squadron to reach the enemy planes while they were still over the water of the English Channel. Flying at well over three hundred miles per hour, everyone in the squadron knew they would engage their foe in minutes.

Looking down, Captain Dawson could see the English coastline pass below. They had achieved the first goal of their mission, that is, to encounter the enemy over the water. While watching the beach pass under the wings of their planes, the pilots in the formation remembered Dawson's motto, "Send them packing before they see land!"

CHAPTER 5

THE FIGHTERS ARE ONLY IN OUR WAY!

"Bandits at two o'clock Captain!" The message in Dawson's headset crackled with a sense of urgency. Dawson recognized the low raspy voice of Lieutenant Collin Mathews. Mathews was flying the right most position in their formation. Quickly looking to his right, Dawson confirmed the young Lieutenant's sighting. Clearing from some light clouds, Dawson counted the enemy planes, seven twin engine Heinkel 111 bombers accompanied by a half dozen Messerschmitt 109 fighters. Flying due west, the German formation was on a heading straight for London, the capital of England.

"Bold as day. Aren't they, Mathews," Captain Dawson called back to the Lieutenant over the radio. Dawson then reminded the entire formation, "Don't forget lads, the bombers are our target, the fighters are only in our way!" As the squadron closed in on the German planes, the

English pilots tensed, waiting for the call from Dawson to attack.

"Line up on me and let's go!" Captain Dawson called to his men and banked right, leading the formation head on into the cluster of enemy planes.

The 14th Squadron swept through the enemy formation, immediately firing on the bombers. In response, the German fighter escort swarmed to protect their comrades. Within seconds, the battle had reached full force. The roaring din of Dawson's engine was interrupted by a multitude of sounds. As enemy fighters were diving and chasing his fellow fighter pilots, the rumble of engines and the repeating crack of machine gun fire echoed all around him. Previously quiet, the radio sparked with messages to and from Dawson's pilots as they maneuvered for position over the enemy fighter planes. Inside the cockpit of his Hurricane, Captain Dawson struggled to concentrate on the mission through the distracting blur of the battle.

Dawson used every trick he knew to try and break past the German fighter escort that protected the deadly bombers. However, it was clear that Dawson and his squadron were flying against some of the enemies' best. So far, every run he made at the bombers ended in quick thinking and smart flying to avoid machine gun fire from the nimble German Me 109 fighters.

Dawson poured on the throttle and pulled back on the stick of his Hurricane in order to increase his altitude. Below, he could see his fellow pilots encountering the same punishing resistance he had.

Throwing the yoke forward, Captain Dawson abruptly ended his climb, and dove for the formation. Dawson's experience taught him that speed can make the difference between a successful run or a disastrous one. Once again, when he approached one of the German bombers, two of the enemy Me 109 fighters met his Hurricane with a rain of bullets. Breaking off before he could get a clear shot at his target, Dawson could see that one of the Me 109s was now stalking him.

CHAPTER 6

THE DANGEROUS GAME

Twisting through the air, the two fighter planes hurled at speeds approaching four hundred miles per hour. Dawson was amazed at the ability of his foe to keep on his tail. At full throttle, the RAF Captain struggled with his controls, trying to out maneuver the German plane. Although he was unable to shake the fighter that pursued him, Dawson's skill as a pilot was, at least, keeping him out of the enemy's gun sights.

"Enough of this!" Captain Dawson barked to himself. Pushing the yoke hard left, Dawson steered his Hurricane back toward the group of German bombers, back to the crowded battle between his men and the enemy aircraft. "If I can't shake you, then I'll lose you in the crowd...," Dawson mumbled to himself as he carefully steered his plane on a dangerous course into the heart of the German air fleet.

Speeding past the battling German and English fighters, and through machine gun fire from the bombers, Dawson rolled and banked ever so close to the other planes. To his right, tracer bullets passed his cockpit, and he rolled hard left to avoid more fire from the sleek Messerschmitt that continued to stalk him.

However, the roll that just saved Dawson from destruction by the Me 109's machine guns, put him on a collision course with one of the menacing Heinkel bombers. Dawson could see the gunner in the German plane frantically pointing and yelling to his commander that there was an English fighter plane hurling straight at them. Instinctively, Dawson again rolled his Hurricane over, and dove earthward to avoid the collision that the German gunner so desperately feared.

Dawson righted his plane and looked up through his cockpit. Above him, he could see the aftermath of his dangerous game. Ironically, the German gunner had less to fear from the English fighter, than the German Me 109 that was immediately behind Dawson's plane. Although

"The roll that just saved Dawson...put him on a collision course..."

Dawson was able to miss the thundering Heinkel 111 bomber, the Me 109 that had so skillfully pursued Dawson, was unable to avoid a mid-air collision. The German fighter pilot's attempt to roll and bank out of the way failed. The Me 109's wing, nearly vertical due to the desperate hard turn, cut into the body of the bomber, shearing off the tail, and crippling both ships. Dawson watched the two German planes lurch and drop from the sky. After the uncontrolled hulks of the two enemy planes passed below his, Dawson noticed two, three, and then four parachutes open and slowly float to the ground.

CHAPTER 7

STILL HEADED FOR LONDON

"Keep on the bombers, lads!" Dawson ordered into his radio. He could see that his pilots were accomplishing their task when the bomber formation began to spread apart. Dawson once more glanced down at the four white parachutes carrying the German fliers, outlined by the green fields below. Startled, Dawson realized that the battle had carried past the coast, and was now over land. The enemy formation was somewhat more ragged, but still headed for London.

Time was growing short for the 14th Squadron as the German bombers neared their target. Surveying the battle in the sky, Captain Dawson noticed his men had been successful at eliminating the enemy fighter planes sent to protect the Heinkels and their devastating cargo.

With the blanket of German fighters gone,

finally the bombers could be targeted.

"Men, form on me!" Captain Dawson shouted into his radio. Dawson then rolled his plane over to begin a looping dive. Joining him, two more Hurricanes followed. Pulling up, and again climbing, Dawson and the two other planes raced to the underside of the westward moving German aircraft. All three fighters unleashed a fury of machine gun fire into the bellies of the enemy bombers. Dawson didn't release the trigger to his eight, wing mounted guns until he and the other two Hurricanes screamed past the formation.

"Again, lads!" shouted Dawson into his radio. When the three RAF fighters rolled over to begin the second pass, two additional members of the squadron were able to join. Like beads on a chain, the planes traced a diving arc, and again climbed to reach the underside of the enemy formation. This time, five Hurricanes fired their weapons at the now hapless, enemy bombers. While the hail of bullets from their combined guns smashed into the Heinkels, Captain Dawson noticed something different. The bomb bay doors of the remaining German aircraft were open.

Straining to look back after his group climbed pass them, he could see one of the twin engine bombers plummeting to the ground below. Two more, with smoke trailing behind, broke formation to bank to the north and east in retreat. Then, twisting to his left, he saw that only four Heinkels were dropping their cargo. As quickly as the bombs released from their perches, the last enemy planes steeply banked to begin their return across the English Channel.

Looking down, Dawson watched dark clouds of smoke rise from the ground where the bombs exploded below. It took almost five seconds for the sound to reach his cockpit due to his altitude over the area. Even though the bombs had been dropped, thankfully, they were falling on empty fields of hay and straw. Dawson and his men had successfully broken up the formation, and forced them north of their target. The few enemy planes that slipped through the 14th Squadron's

defense, ended up dropping their deadly cargo only on abandoned fields instead of the heavily populated city of London.

CHAPTER 8

A ROLL OF STAMPS

Mrs. Winslow called up the staircase to Harry's bedroom, "Harry, it sounds like your cough is getting worse."

Alone in his room, Harry struggled to keep from coughing any further. "I'm fine, Mom, really," Harry claimed, trying to sound as normal as possible with his fever and chills.

Unconvinced, Mrs. Winslow continued to test Harry by pushing him further, "Harry, what are you doing up there?" she asked.

Harry hesitated, and then replied in a scratchy voice, "Writing to Dad!"

Feelings of love, pride, and loneliness washed over Mrs. Winslow at the thought of Harry writing to his father. Before the war, the two were as close as father and son could be. Although Mr. Winslow's commission in the Intelligence Service generally kept him out of harms way in London, he was still away from his family, caught in the middle of a war. Already he had been gone over two years and last saw Harry when he was ten.

"This is such a difficult age for a boy to be away from his father," thought Mrs. Winslow.

"Mom," Harry continued, "can I have some stamps to mail my letters?"

"Certainly, dear," replied Mrs. Winslow, "I'll bring a couple up to you."

"I'll need eight altogether."

Mrs. Winslow shook her head and thought to herself, "That seems like a lot." She grabbed a roll of stamps to be sure there was enough, and climbed the stairs to Harry's room. Opening the door, she handed the stamps to her son.

"Harry, you look pale. Are you sure you're all right?" she asked with a worried voice.

"I'm fine," Harry protested and proceeded to stick the stamps to his envelopes.

A melodic chime from the Winslow's antique grandfather clock announced it was four in the afternoon.

Startled when he realized how late it was, Harry quickly told his mother, "The squadron has already been gone over an hour. I have to get back to the airfield!"

Harry bolted past a surprised Mrs. Winslow and raced down the stairs. Flying down two steps at a time, he ran squarely into his sister, Susan, just as she was starting up the steps.

"Harry Winslow!" Susan scolded her brother. "Where are you going in such a hurry, young man?"

"Sorry, Sis, but I have to get to the airfield," Harry replied with a little bit of apology in his tone. "The squadron should be back any minute!"

Twenty year old Susan had postponed her studies in London to come home to the Winslow farm when her father left to serve his country. To help make ends meet, she took a job on the base as Colonel Harrison's secretary. It also gave her the opportunity to watch over young Harry for her mother.

Susan looked at her little brother for a short moment and in a more gentle voice suggested, "Let's go together. Colonel Harrison asked me to send out some recruitment letters for him, so I was going to work at the base for a couple of hours anyway."

"You mean send out some mail?" Harry questioned.

"Yes, Harry, I have to mail those letters today," replied Susan.

"Just a minute, Sis," Harry said and raced up the stairs. He returned in an instant with eight stamped envelopes. Out of breath and steadying himself on the railing, Harry handed the letters to Susan. "Will you send these with your other mail?" he asked.

"For you, dear Harry Winslow, of course I will," Susan replied.

Pleased his letters would soon be mailed, Harry reached for his coat, while Susan buttoned her sweater. Stepping out of the house, they started for Hampton Airfield.

CHAPTER 9

ALONG THE PATH

Harry and Susan Winslow walked together along the path leading to the RAF base, occasionally stepping over muddy puddles. Although the day had started with beautiful blue skies, it smelled of rain again. The winds had shifted and clouds gathered overhead. Susan tightly held the eight letters in her hand to stop the wind from taking them.

"Did I overhear you tell Mother that you wrote to Father?"

"Yeah," Harry replied, "I told him how all the rain had made the grass in the meadow grow a foot high, and without sheep to graze, it keeps getting higher. Harry paused for a moment and then continued, "I also told him I miss the times he and I used to walk through the fields together and pet the new spring lambs.

You know, I wouldn't even mind it if he'd call me that silly name, 'Sir Harry of Hampton'. Actually, I kind of liked it when he used to tease me with that."

Then Harry blurted, "Oh, Susan, I wish he were here! I want to play with him like we used to. I always felt important when he was with me."

Susan reached out to pull her young brother close to her side and she rumpled his hair.

"I miss him too, Harry. But, we both have to remember that no matter where he is or what he does, we will always be important to him."

Harry managed a faint smile as a shiver ran through his body. The fever was rising and he felt weak from the headache and chills that were overtaking him.

Unaware of Harry's worsening condition, Susan continued to console him. "Father will be pleased to receive eight letters from you all at once!"

Preoccupied with avoiding a deep puddle, Harry mumbled, "Only wrote one to Dad, just mailing the rest for...," Harry abruptly stopped realizing he had said too much.

"Mailing the rest for...who?" Susan questioned.

Hesitating, Harry answered, "Umm...well...

Captain Dawson...asked me if I would mail them."

Susan nodded her head, "That's nice of you to do that for him, Harry. Captain Dawson is pretty important to you, isn't he?"

Harry quickly replied, "He's important to all of us, Sis. In fact, he's probably saving London from attack right now. Without Captain Dawson and the rest of the squadron, Dad..., I mean, people could get hurt."

Susan stopped in her tracks and cut Harry off directly asking, "Is that why those men mean so much to you, Harry? Because they are protecting Father while he's in London? Is that why they're so important?"

Harry and Susan had reached the end of the path. They were at the top of the small hill that looked out over Hampton Airfield. Harry stopped and turned to face Susan. Behind him Susan could see the Operations Building, the maintenance hangers, and the soggy strip of grass that was the launch and return point of the 14th Squadron. Out on the hardstand, the flight crews were assembling in anticipation of the return of Dawson and his pilots.

The look in Harry's eyes told Susan every-

"Because they are protecting father...is that why they're so important?"

thing she wanted to know. But, it also told her to stop asking any more questions. Understanding Harry's desire for privacy about his feelings for the pilots, Susan realized enough had been said.

Stepping forward, she put her hands on his shoulders and turned him towards the airfield.

"Come on, young man," she said in a sympathetic voice. "The squadron will be back soon. Let's get you down to the hardstand."

CHAPTER 10

CONDITION UNKNOWN

The battle with the German formation was over, and it was time for the squadron to return to its home at Hampton Field. Having been in the air for over an hour, and most of that time spent fighting, the planes were low on fuel and ammunition. The pilots were exhausted as well.

"Squadron," Dawson called into his radio, "form up on me." Then he spoke with a little more relaxed tone, "Good work gentlemen, we've sent them packing. Now let's go home!"

Captain Simms was the first to regroup. Bringing his plane alongside Dawson's, Simms waved his hand, and then held up two fingers, signaling two planes shot down. Dawson nodded back, but was more concerned with the sight of a line of bullet holes dotting the fuselage of Simms' Hurricane.

"Andy," Dawson

radioed to Simms, "there are a lot of holes in your plane. Are you okay? What happened?"

Simms keyed his radio, "I got myself in a bit of a row, but things are fine here." Examining Dawson's plane, Simms continued, "Actually Ted, yours would seem to be in a similar condition."

Dawson couldn't see the damage, but he imagined his plane pretty much resembled Simms'. "It was a close call for both of us," Dawson replied.

Through his cockpit canopy, Dawson watched the rest of the planes from the squadron begin to assemble around him. First to line up were the planes that joined in on the sweeping attacks through the bomber formation. Three more Hurricanes, the ones that had been holding off the last of the German fighter escort, joined the group. Finally, Lieutenants Tate and Tomlin returned from chasing the remaining four bombers out over the English Channel.

"Tomlin and I were able to send one more bomber into the drink, Captain!" Lieutenant Tate boasted over the radio to Dawson.

"One less for tomorrow," Dawson replied. "Good work, lads."

No sooner had Dawson acknowledged the return of Tomlin and Tate, when he noticed that Mathews and Hyatt were still missing from the group. "Who's seen Mathews or Hyatt?" Dawson's voice urgently sparked across the radio.

"I saw Hyatt go down over the Channel, Captain." Brian Gainey reported to Dawson.

"Did you see a 'chute' lad?" Dawson asked the young Lieutenant.

"Yes sir, I did." Gainey replied, "I saw his parachute open."

"I saw it too," confirmed another pilot.

"What about Mathews? Did any of you see Mathews go down?" Dawson again asked the rest of the squadron.

"I haven't seen Mathews since we made the coast," said Simms.

"Last I saw of him," began Lieutenant Tomlin, "we were making a run at one of the bombers. I had to break hard right, and he dove. Then I had two bandits on my tail." Tomlin took a heavy breath and finished, "I got a bit busy with the German fighters and lost track of him after that."

Alone in his plane, even the roar of the powerful engine could not drown out the thoughts passing through Dawson's head. "Are the men alive?" he wondered. "Was there anything, anyone could have done? Could they pass over the area and find the downed pilots?"

The responsibility for the men flying in his squadron rested squarely on Dawson's shoulders. It was a responsibility that he was proud to carry. Yet, in times like these, the weight seemed almost unbearable. Dawson knew that by successfully driving off the German bombers, they had saved hundreds of lives. And just as importantly, that ten planes were returning to Hampton, ready to defend England again tomorrow. However, the success of the mission did little to ease the wrenching pain of not knowing what had happened to the two young pilots under his command.

After a long pause over the radio, Dawson summarized the situation in a resigned voice, "Roger. Mathews and Hyatt down. Condition unknown."

The group turned south to return to their airfield. Two spaces in their formation, the ones normally occupied by the missing pilots, remained empty. The radio was silent for the rest of the flight home.

CHAPTER 11

WAITING FOR FURTHER ORDERS

Leading the squadron back to Hampton, Captain Dawson could see clouds gathering on the western horizon. As the formation of Hurricanes approached home, the mid-afternoon sun was blocked out by the building gray clouds. Descending to the airfield, the pilots landed their fighter planes in groups of two, with Captain Simms and the commander, Captain Dawson, touching down last.

Sod and mud tossed into the air when the wheels of Captain Dawson's Hurricane touched the airfield, still soggy from three days of rain. Once on the ground, Dawson throttled up his engine to taxi to the end of the hardstand and lined up with the rest of the squadron. From his cockpit, he could see the ground crews rushing to refuel and rearm the fighter planes. Within minutes of landing, the squadron would be prepared to scramble again to intercept a new wave of enemy aircraft.

However, looking up at the gray sky around him, Dawson was confident that this would probably be the last scramble of the day for his pilots.

Captain Dawson threw back the canopy of his plane and proceeded to climb onto the wing and jump to the ground. No sooner had his feet settled into the wet soil than his flight mechanic, Sergeant Thomas Pendleton was there to meet him.

Sergeant Pendleton greeted Dawson with a pat on the back and in a hearty voice shouted, "Welcome home, sir!"

Dawson responded with merely a nod of his head. Sensing the Captain's dark mood, Pendleton cut short any more conversation and began his customary examination of what he preferred to call "his" Hurricane. It wasn't long before the stocky Sergeant discovered the damage inflicted by the German Me 109s.

"Looking at these holes, I can see it was a wild one today for sure," Pendleton started. "But, with all due respect, Captain, I will have to ask you to take better care of my airplane!"

"I lost two men out there while I was taking care of your blasted airplane!" Dawson snapped at Pendleton's all too familiar sarcastic remark.

Dawson stormed away from the Hurricane, then stopped, and looked back. For just a moment, he watched Pendleton stick his fingers in and out of some of the bullet holes that pierced the airplane. Noticing how close the dotted line of holes came to the cockpit, Dawson simply shook his head, and went off to call Colonel Harrison for further orders.

Standing by the field telephone was Harry Winslow. Harry was allowed on the base as long as he stayed out of the way of the men and safely back from the dangerous airplanes. Day after day, Harry would chat with the brave pilots while they waited to scramble to their planes. Then he faithfully watched for them to return. His love of the men and awe of the fighter planes they flew seemed to keep him on the base almost as much as the pilots. When Dawson reached the phone, Harry couldn't wait to ask him about the mission.

"Did you shoot any..." Harry began to ask.

Abruptly stopping Harry in mid sentence

Captain Dawson barked at the twelve year old Winslow boy, "Blast it, Harry, you could get killed out here. Go home!"

Responding to Dawson's command, a frightened and disappointed Harry Winslow shrank back, and ran for the hedgerow fence at the end of the hardstand. Choking back tears, Harry's slight frame slipped through the small gap in the hedge and back to the Winslow side.

Captain Dawson grabbed the field telephone to call Colonel Harrison. While waiting for the Colonel to answer, he watched Harry run along

the path that led back to the Winslow house.

Gathering behind the line of Hurricanes on the hardstand, the remaining pilots of the 14th Fighter Squadron awaited their new orders. If the Germans continued sending flights of bombers, the tired pilots would immediately scramble back into the air.

Attempting to relieve the tension, Captain Simms commented, "Relax gentlemen, the weather will stop the Germans before we have to. Besides, look at Ted. If Headquarters needed us to scramble again, he would be off the phone by now."

Simms and the other men could see Dawson still talking on the field telephone. Dawson's conversation with Colonel Harrison would either send them back to the sky, or back to their quarters. They all watched as Dawson nodded his head and made some gestures with his free hand. Everyone could read Dawson's lips as he finished the conversation with, "Yes sir!" and slammed down the phone. The nine pilots rose to their feet and gathered in a tight circle when Captain Dawson approached. Dawson, seeing the impatience in his pilots' eyes, lengthened his stride to meet the anxious men that much quicker.

Holding his hands up, Dawson cut the tension by quickly announcing to the pilots, "Quarters lads! There's more rain gathering, and we're ordered to stand down."

A wave of relief washed over the group. Together, the ten pilots turned to leave the field and let the mechanics make the necessary repairs to their Hawker Hurricanes. By tomorrow, all ten planes, plus two reserve fighters, needed to be combat ready.

CHAPTER 12

THE BRIEFING ROOM

After every mission, the pilots would meet in the briefing room of the Operations Building to review the day's events. Today, while the other pilots discussed the details of the flight and the ensuing battle with the intelligence officers, Captain Dawson impatiently waited to hear word of the two pilots downed during the scuffle.

"Ted," Colonel Harrison called to Captain Dawson, "clever move coming up through the middle of the formation like that."

"Thank you, Colonel." replied Dawson in a disinterested tone. "We were running out of time as they approached London. It was the only thing I could think of to push them off course a bit."

Colonel Harrison shook his head and went on, "A bit, Ted? You pushed them twelve miles to the north. The most those bombers hit was a bale of hay and an abandoned ox cart. Overall, good show, gentlemen. Good show indeed!"

Having received all the information he

needed, Colonel Harrison closed his notebook and got up from his chair. "It looks like we'll be standing down for some time with this new storm." Harrison then leaned over and quietly said to Dawson in a reassuring tone, "We'll hear about Hyatt and Mathews soon enough."

Captain Dawson looked at the Colonel and nodded his head.

Making his way to the door, Harrison called to the pilots, "Rest as best you can, there's surely more to come." And then he closed the door behind him.

Even though Colonel Harrison had left, the men continued discussing the battle, searching for clues to when, where and how their two fellow pilots were downed. Captain Dawson worked his way around the room to congratulate each of his men for a job well done, and provide what insight he could regarding the missing pilots. And yet, however sincere the praise was from Colonel Harrison and Captain Dawson, to the rest of the men, it felt unwarranted in the absence of Hyatt and

Mathews. The RAF pilots were a family. Any harm that came to any one of them was felt by all.

Pulling the zipper of his jacket closer to his chin, Dawson left the briefing room and stepped outside of the Operations Building into the cool, misty evening.

CHAPTER 13

WONDERFUL NEWS

While walking back to his quarters, Dawson was stopped by a young Corporal and Colonel Harrison's secretary, Susan Winslow.

"Captain Dawson," Susan called out as she approached him, "we have wonderful news."

"Yes, Captain, great news," agreed the Corporal, somewhat out of breath. "I was just informed over the wire that the coast guard picked up Mathews and Hyatt."

"Colonel Harrison immediately sent us to tell you," said Susan. Holding up a piece of paper, she continued, "Here, read it for yourself."

Captain Dawson took the note from Susan and read the message aloud, "Lieutenants Mathews and Hyatt picked up by Coastal Command. Pilots to be returned to Hampton in the morning."

Dawson stopped reading and looked at the other two, "Now that is great news! You know, tomorrow should be a fine day!"

"But, Captain, tomorrow's forecast predicts

continued rain and fog all day long. How can that make it a fine day?" the Corporal asked a bit confused.

"In times like these, lad," Dawson replied in a fatherly tone, "a rainy day will definitely make it a fine day."

The Corporal shrugged his shoulders and quietly turned away, without a clue of the tremendous weight that had just been lifted from Dawson's shoulders.

After an awkward silence, Susan asked, "Captain Dawson, did you know this letter needed two stamps?"

Confused, Dawson just looked at Susan.

"I'm sorry, Captain," she explained, "I meant to say, I mailed the other letters you gave to Harry, but this one needed two stamps so I couldn't send it out."

Dawson took the letter, too distracted to pay much attention and stuffed it into his pocket. Then he turned to Susan.

"Susan," he started, "have you seen Harry

around? I need to talk to him."

"I saw him running home just a bit ago," she replied.

Captain Dawson stood motionless, thinking of what to do. Absorbed in the loss of his pilots, he felt ashamed for snapping at Harry when the squadron returned. Dawson desperately wanted to apologize for his sharpness and hoped Harry would be around. In fact, Dawson realized this was one of the few times Harry wasn't underfoot.

"Is there something you want me to tell him?" Susan asked.

"No," Dawson replied, "I really need to tell him myself."

Susan could sense the urgency in Captain Dawson and offered, "I'm leaving to go home now. If you would like to come with me and see him, it would probably be all right."

Dawson nodded his head. "If that's agreeable with your mother, I would like to see him now."

CHAPTER 14

THE MYSTERY IS SOLVED

Susan and Captain Dawson walked along the still muddy path from Hampton Airfield to the Winslow house. Evening had settled in and the cloudy gray sky grew even darker. The chill air felt damp and Susan pulled her sweater close.

Poor at making idle conversation, Captain Dawson struggled to find something to talk about with Susan. Noticing the Winslow home silhouetted against the darkening sky, he awkwardly complimented, "Your family is following the 'blackout' rules very well by closing the shutters on your windows."

Susan was amazed at the Captain's shyness, in stunning contrast to his manner as a fighter pilot. "Yes, thank you," she replied. "It's important for everyone's safety."

Reaching the house and stepping inside,

Susan introduced Captain Dawson to Mrs. Winslow. Mrs. Winslow was excited to have a celebrity in her home, but even more important to her was that one of Harry's beloved pilots was here to visit him. Harry talked constantly about the twelve pilots in the 14th Squadron, and Mrs. Winslow recognized the tall, good-looking Captain Dawson from Harry's descriptions.

"Good evening, Mrs. Winslow," Dawson said politely. "I wonder if I may have a few words with Harry?"

"I sent him to bed earlier," explained Mrs. Winslow. "He fell sick today with a fever after being out in this damp weather. But, I think a few minutes chatting with you would be all right and probably do him a world of good. Ever since he came home, he's been quite gloomy."

The memory of the afternoon's encounter with Harry washed over Dawson and he set his mouth into a grim line. Turning toward the landing, Susan and her mother led him up the stairs to Harry's room. With a quick knock, Captain Dawson strode through the door. A pale and feverish Harry Winslow struggled to rise up in his bed. Feeling as if he were dreaming, and completely amazed at the sight of the RAF pilot in his room, Harry fought hard to say something.

"Captain...Captain Dawson," Harry stuttered, "ahh... please... sit... please sit down."

Dawson sat down in a small chair at the side of Harry's bed. Tired from the fever, Harry laid back and rested his damp head on the pillow. Captain Dawson looked at Harry and began his apology.

"Harry," Dawson said in a quiet voice, "I lost two planes up there today."

Unaware of what had happened during the mission, Harry was surprised and saddened by the news. Judging by the look on Dawson's face, Harry worried that he was the cause of even more trouble on the airfield and wondered how he would be punished. Pushing his head further into his pillow, Harry fought back tears.

Dawson could see he unknowingly upset Harry, and quickly continued, "But the pilots, Hyatt and Mathews, are both all right. In fact, they will be back here at Hampton tomorrow morning."

"Oh, thank goodness," Harry said through his pillow, still fighting back the tears.

"The worst thing that happened today was that..." Dawson struggled for the words.

Searching for the right thing to say, he surveyed Harry's room. Trying to arrange his thoughts, he rose from the chair and shuffled over to a tall dresser beside the window that overlooked

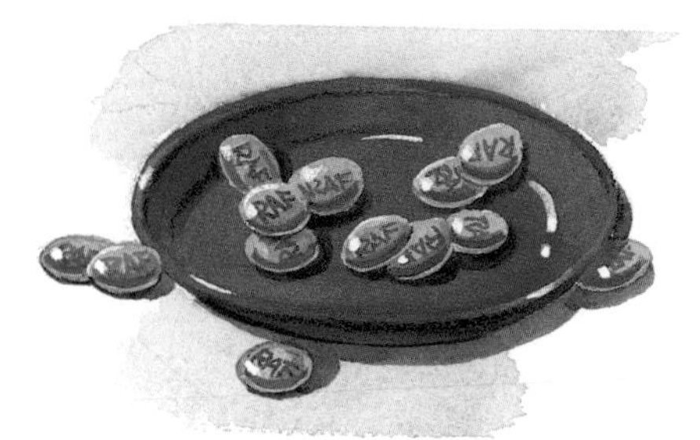

Hampton Airfield. On the dresser top, Dawson saw a homemade model airplane, some toy soldiers and a dish filled with buttons.

As his eyes scanned the items on the dresser, Dawson continued, "The worst thing was that I snapped..."

Then he noticed that next to the dish lay a small sewing kit, a scissor and a roll of stamps. Dawson reached for the dish, but in doing so knocked it over, scattering the buttons across the floor. As he went to pick them up, he noticed they were Royal Air Force uniform buttons. Retrieving the last one from the floor beside the dresser, he saw a shoeshine kit in a small wooden box. Next to the box, carefully placed on newspaper, were a pair of regulation RAF dress shoes shined to a sparkle.

Distracted by his observations, Dawson's train of thought was completely derailed.

Instantly, Captain Dawson realized Harry Winslow was the one responsible for all the secret favors he and his men had enjoyed. Harry had shined his pilots' shoes, cleaned up their quarters, sewed his buttons, and even mailed his letters.

"Captain, Captain Dawson?" Harry asked, "Are you all right?"

"Yes, Harry, I'm fine," Dawson responded in a much softer tone. Finally realizing what he wanted to tell Harry, he continued, "I came here to tell you that I'm sorry I snapped at you today out on the hardstand. But as Squadron Leader it is my responsibility to make sure all my pilots are as safe as possible."

"Yes sir, I understand," Harry returned in a disappointed voice.

"Now currently I am missing three members of my squadron," Dawson continued in a firm voice. "Two will be returned tomorrow. The other one would be well advised to join us as soon as he can."

A confused Harry Winslow looked up from his pillow and asked, "Who is the other pilot? You told me you only lost two."

Dawson stepped back to Harry's bed and

bent down to speak in his ear, "The other one is you, Mr. Harry Winslow. When you're well again, I expect to see you on the hardstand."

Harry and Captain Dawson looked at each other in silence for a long moment. Harry felt a sense of surprise and relief, as well as a hint of pride, as he tried to put his thoughts together.

Then Dawson broke the silence and said, "I need to return to the airfield, Harry. I hope to see you there soon."

As the Captain stepped out of the room, Harry called, "Yes sir, as soon as I'm able!"

Barely capable of controlling his excitement, Harry settled into his bed for the night. Laying there in the dark, he felt warm, and not just from the fever. For the first time, Harry realized that he was important to Captain Dawson.

Susan and Mrs. Winslow saw Dawson to the door. He left the warm Winslow house and stepped outside into the cold, damp night. Thunder rumbled over the English countryside while he followed the path leading back to Hampton Airfield. On his way, he thought of young Harry and the things he'd seen in his bedroom. An old habit, Dawson put his hand in his coat pocket where he felt the letter Susan had given him, the letter that needed another stamp.

Finally reaching the end of the path, Dawson stepped through the gap in the hedge, back onto Hampton Airfield. A flash of lightning arced through the sky, briefly illuminating the Hawker Hurricanes on the hardstand and the rest of the airfield. In that moment, he became aware of something else, something even greater than solving the mystery of the favors. For the first time, Captain Dawson realized just how important he was to Harry Winslow.

IN HINDSIGHT

In September of 1939, Germany's military used the combination of superior air power and mobile land forces to invade Poland. Their "Blitzkrieg" (lightning war) tactics proved so successful that by the following spring most of the European mainland had been conquered.

Standing on the coastal hills of occupied France in May of 1940, German commanders spied the white cliffs of Dover reflected in the waters of the English Channel. England would be the next target of the unstoppable German forces.

Map of English Channel area

Their plan for invading Britain, called Operation Sea Lion, required the destruction of the British Royal Air Force by the pilots and planes of the German Luftwaffe. After eliminating the RAF, the Luftwaffe could control the skies over England, enabling German ground forces to cross the channel and invade with little opposition.

Preparing for an invasion that September, Germany

Coastal radar station

launched their air offensive designed to crush British resistance, from hastily built bases in France. Starting in June, waves of German Heinkel and Dornier bombers, escorted by Messerschmitt fighters, flew across the English Channel to attack British shipping and military installations. England bravely defended itself by sending fighter squadrons of the Royal Air Force to stop the onslaught of German planes.

Britain's defense relied on two key elements. First, an advanced radar station network that could locate incoming enemy aircraft while they were still over the English Channel. And second, the ability of the RAF squadrons, strategically scattered throughout the English countryside, to "scramble" their fighters at a moment's notice in order to intercept advancing enemy planes.

Using radar and observers, the RAF's air-raid early-warning system could detect German aircraft formations assembling over the French coast, while they were still twenty-five minutes flying time away from England. Once spotted, Fighter Command alerted their squadrons to the attack and the skilled RAF pilots would "scramble" their fighters within minutes. The British planes needed fifteen

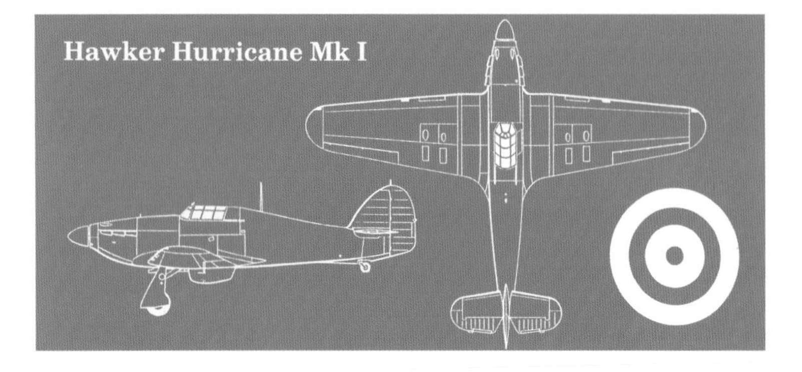

minutes to reach 20,000 feet, approximately the same altitude as the German formation. When things worked right, the RAF fighters were able to intercept the enemy several minutes before they reached the English coast.

Although the Luftwaffe possessed greater numbers of aircraft and experienced pilots than the RAF, they soon found themselves at a disadvantage. The German planes were generally designed for short to medium range missions, with limited fuel capacity. The amount consumed simply to fly to England and safely return to France left little reserve for combat over English soil. On the other hand, RAF planes expended relatively little fuel flying to intercept, allowing the English pilots more time in the air to fight.

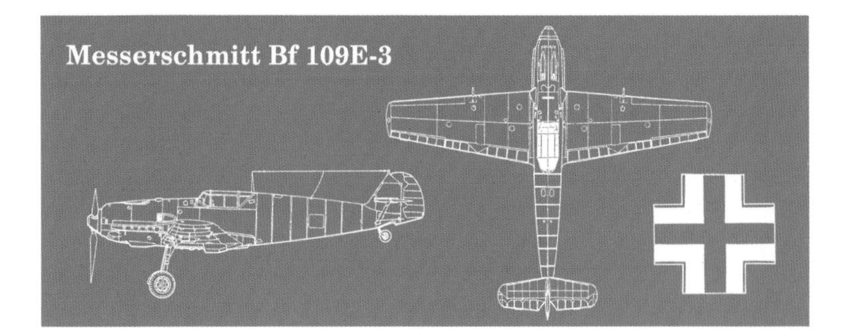

Another advantage for the RAF, their planes could quickly return to the airfield, refuel, rearm and scramble back into the sky in minutes.

The fight for air superiority over England, originally planned as the first step to invasion, would become the battle itself. In the summer months of 1940, during what would later be known as the Battle of Britain, RAF pilots took to their Hurricane and Spitfire fighter planes hour after hour, day after day. Between missions, pilots tried their best to relax, but the tension of waiting for the next "scramble" could be almost as exhausting as combat. The routine of an RAF fighter pilot caught in this five month battle is vividly retold:

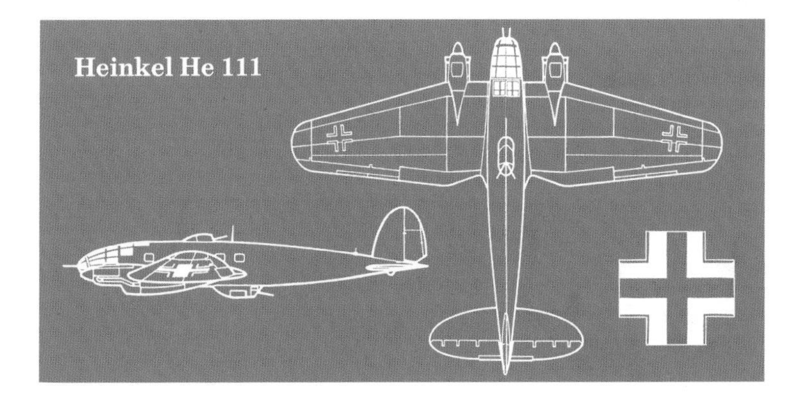

"Fighter pilots were typically being called upon to fly at least three sorties a day, and this figure would only rise as Luftwaffe raids grew both in size and intensity.

An indication of just how hectic the daily schedule was... can be gauged by the following quote from No. 501 Squadron ace, Flight Lieutenant Eustace "Gus" Holden;

'At dawn one day, the squadron went to 30,000 feet and, on landing, I started to walk to the mess for some breakfast when I was recalled for standby. Relieved ten minutes later, I again made for the mess, but just as I got to the door, I was called back and I had to go to 30,000 feet again. Back at the aerodome in due course, I tried to get another meal. I was half way through it when I was wanted for another standby. When that came to nothing, I made for my quarters to have a shave. I'd just lathered myself when the loud speaker called, "501 Squadron-readiness". So up to 30,000 feet again. Later I finished shaving and actually had time for lunch before being called for another standby. Then about five o'clock, at 30,000 feet again for the fourth time that day.'"

Hawker Hurricanes scrambling from their airfield.

Ferociously fighting the attacking Luftwaffe, by the end of October 1940, the courageous RAF pilots and their support crews, had so successfully defended their homeland, that Germany was forced to scrap their plans for an invasion of Britain that year. British Prime Minister Winston Churchill expressed the gratitude of the English people for the heroic efforts of the Royal Air Force when he said, "Never was so much, owed by so many, to so few."

Although the Battle of Britain had been won, the war was still far from over. The powerful German air force continued to regularly launch attacks against England's airfields, supply lines, and coastal cities in attempts to disrupt the British, and allied, military machine. RAF pilots continued to "scramble" to protect their homeland for the remaining years of World War 2.

GLOSSARY

Barracks: Buildings used by military personnel.

Captain: A military officer ranking below colonel and above lieutenant.

Colonel: A military officer ranking below general and above captain.

Fuselage: The central body of an airplane.

Hardstand: A hard surface area next to an airstrip used for parking planes and ground vehicles.

Hawker Hurricane: A type of British fighter plane.

Hedgerow: A row of bushes or small trees that form a fence.

Heinkel 111: A type of German bomber (also He 111).

Intercept: To stop or interrupt the progress of enemy aircraft.

Lieutenant: A military officer ranking below captain.

Messerschmitt 109: A type of German fighter plane (also Me 109).

Operations Building: The airfield's central administration building.

Quarters: Housing for officers.

Radar: Radio Detecting And Ranging. An electronic method of detecting distant objects and determining their position.

Stick or Yoke: The control lever of an airplane used for steering.